THE WOLFHOUND

by KRISTINE L. FRANKLIN

paintings by KRIS WALDHERR

LOTHROP, LEE & SHEPARD BOOKS
NEW YORK

To my sister Linda
—K.F.

For Jennifer, Chris, and Colton Johnson
—K.W.

The illustrator wishes to thank Russ Mitkowski, Barbara Skinner of Sky Run Borzoi, Lauraine Anne Pell, and Rancho Gabriel Rapture "Aleksandra" for their help with this book. Thanks also to Ron Mitkowski, Martha Siegel, Letecia Stewart, Officer Ingrid R. Stokner of Brooklyn Mounted New York City Park Enforcement, and Kensington Stables.

Printed in the United States of America.

First Edition   1 2 3 4 5 6 7 8 9 10

Production supervision by Bonnie King

The text was set in Carolina. Printed and bound by Worzalla.

The illustrations in this book were done in watercolor and oil paints on watercolor paper

Library of Congress Cataloging in Publication Data

Franklin, Kristine L. The wolfhound / by Kristine L. Franklin; illustrated by Kris Waldherr.
p.   cm. Summary: Pavel saves the life of the enormous dog he finds half-frozen in the snow, but since only the tsar and the nobles are allowed to keep wolfhounds, Pavel fears he will be punished for stealing. ISBN 0-688-13674-5. — ISBN 0-688-13675-3 (lib bdg.) [1. Dogs—Fiction. 2. Russia—Fiction.] I. Waldherr, Kris, ill. II. Title. PZ7.F85922Wo   1995   [E]—dc20   94-14595   CIP   AC

P AVEL FOUND THE DOG the day his father went to town to
sell butter.

In the morning the sky was as blue as the sapphires in
the Tsarina's wedding necklace. By noon it was heavy and
gray, and soon the snowflakes were sifting down, covering
the ground like white sugar on a rich man's tea cake. By
suppertime the wind was howling across the chimney, and
still his father had not come home, so Pavel trudged
through the storm to milk the cows alone.

When he got to the barn, Pavel heard a whimper.

The snowflakes whirled about, stinging his eyes, sticking to the warm place on the scarf wrapped tight across his face. He dropped both buckets and plunged his arms into the snow. At the bottom of the drift, where the dead grass poked through, lay a half-frozen dog.

Pavel dragged the heavy animal into the barn. With stiff fingers he lit a candle. Then he brushed the snow from the dog's fur and rubbed its sides with his hands. The dog opened its great brown eyes and thumped its tail once.

Then Pavel remembered the cows and milked them both quickly, pouring some of the milk into a wooden bowl. He left the bowl by the dog's nose, patted it on the head, and carried the buckets of milk to the house.

The next morning, after the last snowflake had fluttered out of the tired sky, Pavel's father came home. When Pavel told him about the dog, they went to the barn to see it.

"It was almost dead," said Pavel, "but I saved it. May I keep it?" He pushed open the barn door and gasped. There in the shadows stood the most beautiful dog Pavel had ever seen.

"A wolfhound!" whispered Pavel's father. "Only nobles and dukes and the Tsar himself keep wolfhounds. They will say you stole it." The fear in his voice made Pavel shiver. "You should have left this dog to die."

"I couldn't," stammered Pavel. "Perhaps there will be a reward."

"Prison will be the only reward," growled his father, "or worse." He scratched his beard thoughtfully. "After dark I will drive the dog away. If it dies, it dies. We will never tell a soul that it was here." He turned and hurried back to the house.

The wolfhound stood watching Pavel. Its pointed nose stretched forward, sniffing the frosty air between them. For an instant their eyes met. What a crime it would be to let such a wonderful creature die in the freezing night!

Pavel tied a piece of rope around the dog's neck. Then he led it out of the barn and across the snowy pasture, toward the low stone wall that surrounded the Tsar's vast private forest.

By the time they reached the wall, Pavel's heart was pounding. Those who crossed these icy gray stones, those who dared enter the Tsar's forest, did not often return. Besides the gamekeepers with their guns, the forest was full of wild boars, bears, and wolves. Pavel hesitated. His heart thundered in his chest. He stared at the dark trees standing like solemn soldiers in the snow. Then he looked at the dog and scrambled over the wall. He jerked the rope, and the wolfhound sprang nimbly over after him.

Pavel fumbled with the knot, glancing all around, listening, waiting for something dreadful to happen. The wolfhound pranced about, panting in Pavel's face and smacking its tail against his legs.

"Sit still!" cried Pavel, and the wolfhound sat quietly, as if by magic. Pavel untied the rope and showed it to the dog.

"You're free, see?" he said. "Now go. Run home."

"Go!" said Pavel. "Go! Before they find me here and arrest me for a thief."

The dog didn't move.

The dog wagged its tail.

Pavel swung the rope around his head. "Go home!" he shouted. But the wolfhound only leapt back over the wall, out of the Tsar's forest, and barked.

Pavel climbed over to fetch the dog. "Do you want to freeze to death?" he cried. Angry tears stung his eyes. The wolfhound leaned against him, its tail swishing in the snow. Pavel put both arms around the dog's neck and buried his face in its fur. Then he tied the rope around its neck again, coaxed it over the wall, and headed into the forest without looking back.

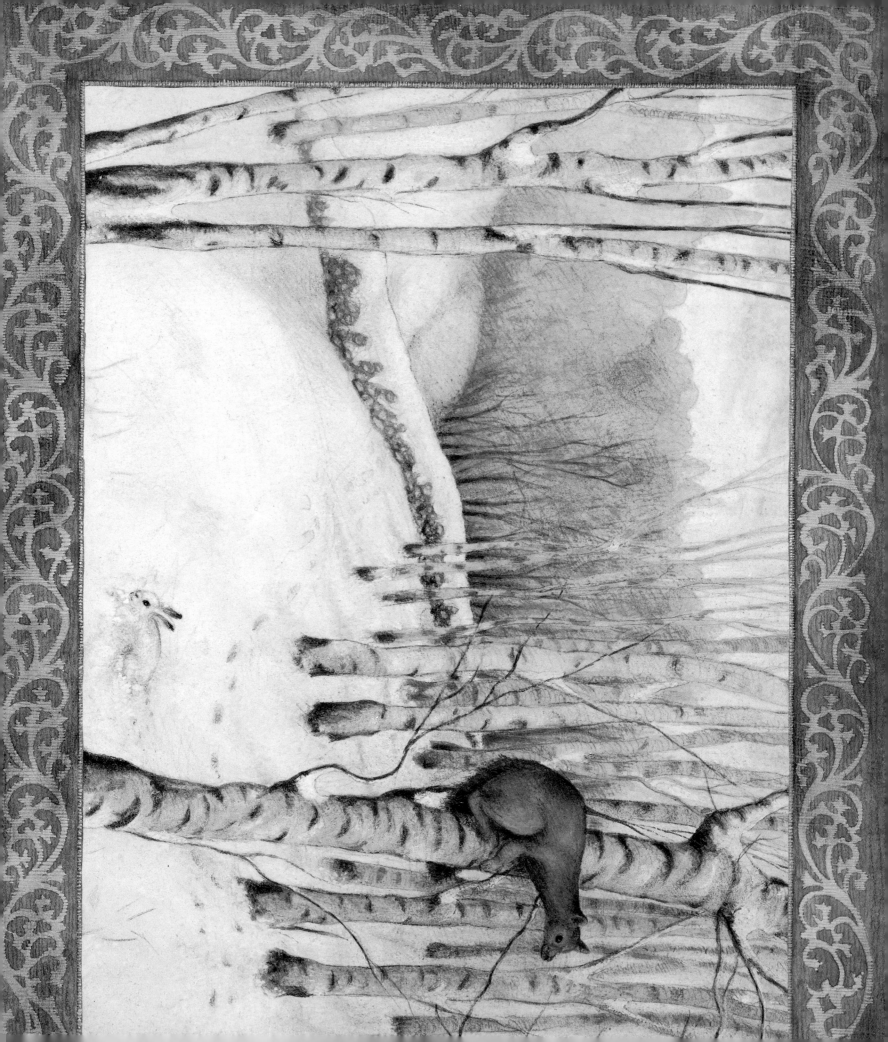

The forest was as silent as an empty church. The sun shone bright between the shadows of the gaunt, bare birch trees, and Pavel soon stopped fretting about the gamekeepers and the wild beasts. But the snow was deep and cold and soft. Pavel's hands and feet began to ache and his eyes burned.

"You can find your way home from here," he told the dog, and leaned over to unfasten the rope.

Suddenly the wolfhound growled deep in its throat. It sniffed the air, pointing its long nose toward a nearby stand of trees. Pavel stared at the shadowy, shaggy beasts running across the snow.

"Wolves," he whispered, and his heart began to thunder in his chest.

The big dog strained against the rope as the wolves moved closer—close enough for Pavel to see their yellow eyes.

Then the wolfhound lunged, jerking the rope from Pavel's hand. With slow, careful steps it approached the wolves. They froze in their tracks, and then, without a sound, turned and melted between the trees. The wolfhound lifted its head and barked twice.

"Where did you get that dog?" asked a loud voice. Pavel whirled to face a man on horseback. The man had a black beard and wore a black fur hat. His blue eyes were as cold as stone.

"I found it," said Pavel. His mouth was dry and he shivered, but not because he was cold.

"Where?" asked the man.

Pavel swallowed hard. "Outside our barn." He spoke carefully, willing his voice not to tremble. "It was nearly frozen. I gave it milk." His father's words echoed in his head: "Prison . . . or worse."

"This dog is mine," said the man, patting the dog on the head as it waggled with joy beside him. "You're a wretched beast, Tata," he scolded. And then he did a surprising thing. He smiled.

"What is your name, boy?"

"Pavel, son of Ivan the milkman," mumbled Pavel through numb lips.

"I thank you, Pavel Ivanovich," said the man, "for saving my wicked, wandering Tatiana from a frosty death." He removed a glove and extended his hand to Pavel. Pavel tugged off one woolen mitten and shook the man's hand. That was when he saw the ring. The Tsar's own ring. Pavel stared at the ring and swallowed hard.

"Can you find your way home from here?" asked the Tsar. Pavel looked up. The Tsar's face was kind, and his blue eyes laughed at Pavel above red cheeks.

Pavel grinned and nodded. Then he spun around, plowed back through the snow, and ran all the way home.

Pavel told everyone the story of Tatiana the wolfhound, how he had saved her life, how she had saved him from wolves, and how the Tsar himself had thanked him. But no one believed his story, not even his father.

Then one day, when the birch trees had buds the size of a chicken's beak, there came a knock at the door. Outside stood a royal messenger with a letter in his hand. A crowd of villagers was gathered behind him.

"A gift," said the messenger. "From the Tsar." Everyone began to talk at once until a servant stepped through the crowd and set a huge basket at Pavel's feet. The crowd fell silent, and even the melting snow stopped dripping from the eaves, as if to see what would happen next.

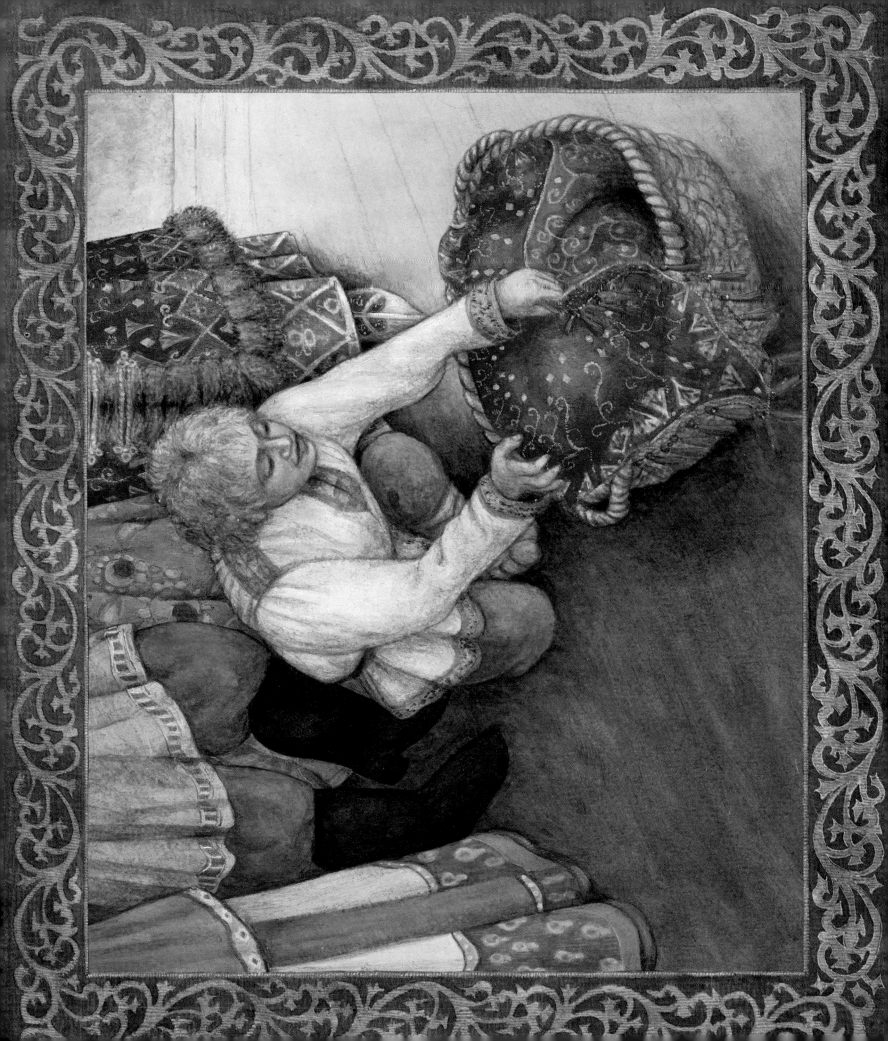

Pavel lifted the cloth that covered the basket. An enormous white and brown puppy jumped into his lap. Pavel gathered the pup in his arms and held it close. The villagers pressed in around them, eager to touch the marvelous rare creature, the borzoi, whose name means "speed"—the wolfhound, dog of the tsars.

The messenger opened the letter and held it high for everyone to see. In the center of the page was a large inky pawprint. The messenger cleared his throat.

"Tatiana," he read in a loud, official voice, "sends her love."